Pilot Ollie & Pilot Polly's
Amazing Adventures

www. planecharacters.com

Plane Characters Ltd ©

Passport Hunt!
See if you can
find all the
passports.

It's a lovely day when Pilot Ollie and Pilot Polly arrive at work. The sun is shining, the birds are singing and it's a perfect day to go flying.

Today we are going to follow Pilot Ollie and Pilot Polly, have a look around the plane and the flight deck where they work.

The pilots report to the briefing room. "Good morning Woody," says Pilot Polly.

Woody Weatherman is in charge of the weather forecasts for the whole world and produces weather maps for all the pilots. It's important for pilots to know where they might meet bad weather such as thunderstorms.

Pilots steer their planes around thunderstorms as they can make the flight really bumpy.

Also Pilot Ollie and Pilot Polly need to know what the weather is like at their destination so they can tell their passengers.

While Pilot Ollie and Pilot Polly are looking at the weather maps, Chris Controller strolls in. His job is to plan the route the plane takes to its destination.

He produces maps and draws a big red line on them so the pilots know where to go. Chris Controller also works in the control tower, a very tall building from where he can see the whole airport through the windows. We will follow him to work on another day.

Chris Controller wears a headset with a microphone and speaks on the radio to all the pilots in their planes. The pilots all wear headsets with microphones too so they can talk back.

Chris Controller tells them where to go on the ground and gives them permission to start their engines, take off and land. He can control lots of planes at the same time.

Once Pilot Ollie and Pilot Polly have seen the weather and the route to their destination they decide how much fuel they will need for the flight.

They put all of the weather maps and charts into their flight cases.

Chris Controller will phone Freddie Fueler at the fuel company to tell them how much fuel to put on the plane. The fuel is pumped into the plane from a tanker lorry and stored in the plane's wings.

Just like the passengers, Pilot Ollie and Pilot Polly have to go through security before they go to the plane. They take their computers out of their bags and put them through the X-ray scanner.

The security officers make sure that nothing dangerous is taken on the plane. Pilot Ollie and Pilot Polly walk through the metal detector which sometimes go BEEP. If it beeps they get searched by the security officers.

Pilot Ollie and Pilot Polly meet up with the cabin crew and walk out to their plane which is shining brightly in the sunshine.

Alfie Engineer is waiting to meet them. "Morning Alfie," says Pilot Polly. "Is the plane ready to fly?"

Alfie Engineer has checked the plane's engines and topped them up with oil. "Yes, she's all ready for you Captain," he says.

Alfie Engineer knows everything about how the planes work. We will follow him at work one day and learn how a plane flies.

Before they go flying all pilots walk around their planes and have a good look at them.

Pilot Ollie puts his flight case in the flight deck and then takes a walk around the plane. He looks at all the probes and sensors, the wings and the tail.

He has a good look at the engines, the wheels and brakes. It's important that the wheels and brakes are in good condition as the plane travels at over one hundred miles an hour when it takes off and lands.

The engines have big spinning fans at the front that suck air in. Once the air is inside the engine, fuel is mixed in, a spark sets it on fire and hot air blasts out the back of the engine.

The hot blasting air is called thrust and makes the engines **ROOOOAAAARRRR**.

The thrust pushes the plane forward on the ground and in the air. When the engines are running Alfie Engineer makes sure that nobody goes near them.

In the airport terminal building the passengers are checking in.

They give their suitcases to the check in staff and they then speed off on conveyor belts through the terminal building and end up on baggage trucks.

Larry Loader drives the baggage trucks, takes the suitcases out to the plane and loads them into the plane's cargo hold. "Morning Larry," says Pilot Ollie as he finishes his walk round checks.

Pilot Ollie and Pilot Polly take their seats in the flight deck. They put their flight cases with their maps in down beside their seats.

The flight deck is full of computer screens, lights, switches and dials. It takes new pilots months to learn what every switch does.

It's quite small in the flight deck as Pilot Polly and Pilot Ollie need to reach all the switches and instruments from their seat. If the flight deck was too big, they wouldn't be able to reach them!

In front of Pilot Ollie and Pilot Polly's seats are the plane's controls. The control wheel looks like the steering wheel of a car but it's mounted on a pole.

It works just like a steering wheel and if you turn it left, the plane will turn left. Turn the control wheel to the right and the plane will turn to the right.

When you pull the control wheel towards you the plane goes up and pushing it away from you makes the plane go down.

There are two pedals by Pilot Ollie and Pilot Polly's feet. They help turn the plane in the air and help steer the plane on the ground.

Pushing the left pedal forward will turn the plane left. The tops of the pedals work the planes brakes.

When Pilot Ollie or Pilot Polly push down with their toes the brakes come on and the plane slows down.

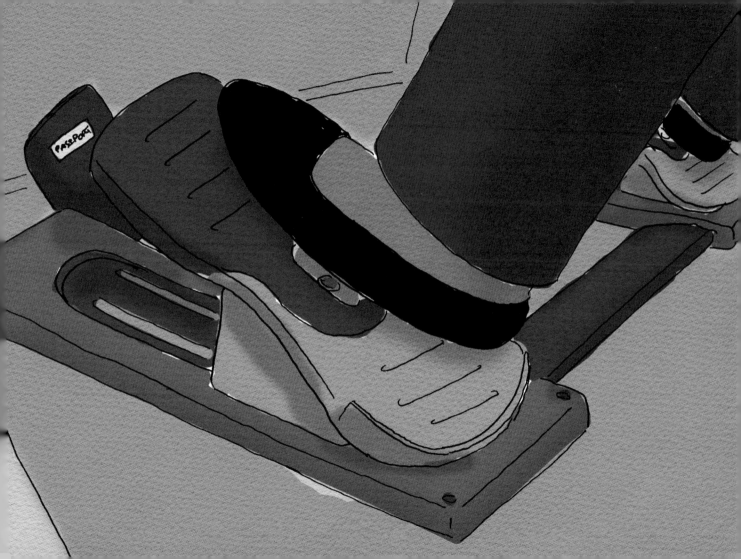

By Pilot Ollie's and Pilot Polly's seats are the engine thrust levers. They control how fast the engines are running and how much thrust they produce.

Pushing the thrust levers forward adds more fuel, increases the power of the engines and makes the plane go faster.

As the thrust increases the **ROOOAAARRR** noise from the engines gets louder. You will hear this as the plane takes off.

Soon all the suitcases are onboard, the wings are full of fuel and Pilot Ollie and Pilot Polly have finished programming the plane's computers.

A bus carrying all the passengers arrives, they climb up the steps onto the plane and take their seats.

All of the plane's doors are closed and Pilot Polly talks on the radio to Chris Controller. "You are cleared to taxi to the runway and take off," says Chris Controller.

On the runway Pilot Ollie pushes the engine thrust levers forward.

The engines **ROOOAAARRR** as the plane gets faster and faster. When it reaches take off speed Pilot Ollie gently pulls back on his control column and the plane leaps into the air.

Pilot Polly reaches forwards and moves a lever that looks like a wheel on a stick. Moving the lever up moves the plane's wheels up. They are stored safely until they are needed again when the plane lands.

There is a computer with a keyboard down by Pilot Ollie and Pilot Polly's knees. It works just like a sat-nav in a car.

Before taking off Pilot Ollie and Pilot Polly program the computer with the route to their destination.

It's the route that Chris Controller gave them in the briefing room. Now that they are flying they can change the route to go around the thunderstorms on Woody Weatherman's maps. Flying through storm clouds would make the flight very bumpy.

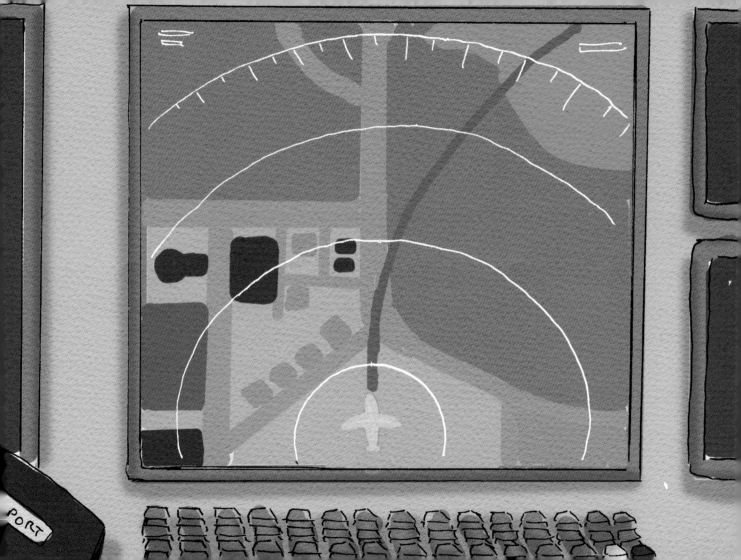

In front of Pilot Ollie and Pilot Polly are two more computer screens.

The one on the outside shows how fast the plane is going and also how high it is in the sky. This height is called its altitude.

In the middle of the screen is a circle which is half brown and half blue. When Pilot Ollie and Pilot Polly fly through the clouds, they can't see out of the windows so they use this circle to fly the plane. The brown half is the ground and the blue half is the sky.

The second big computer screen that Pilot Ollie and Pilot Polly look at shows them a map of the route to their destination.

The map shows what's under the plane and what's ahead of it such as mountains and sea. The pilots can press a switch and show the weather on this screen so they can fly around those big bumpy thunderstorms.

Once the plane is flying the pilots can use the autopilot to help them.

The autopilot is a computer that follows the route that Pilot Ollie and Pilot Polly have programmed in. It would be very tiring if they had to fly all the way by themselves.

The plane cruises at over 500 miles an hour and at nearly 40,000 feet high. The cabin crew look after the passengers and serve them drinks and snacks. On some planes the passengers can watch movies or a map of where they are.

Before long it's almost time to land. Pilot Ollie and Pilot Polly pull back on the thrust levers, the engines quietly slow down and the plane glides down towards the landing runway.

It takes about twenty minutes to get back on the ground. Pilot Ollie and Pilot Polly speak to the controllers to find out which runway to land on.

As the plane makes its approach Pilot Ollie and Pilot Polly need to slow the plane down. To help them they have a speedbrake lever in the flight deck. When Pilot Ollie pulls the lever, doors on the top of the wings open and stick up into the air.

This helps the plane slow down. There is another lever in the flightdeck called flaps. As the plane slows down Pilot Polly moves the flap lever, extra sections of wing extend and the wing gets bigger. This helps it fly slower ready for landing.

Just before they land Pilot Polly pushes the wheel lever down and the plane's wheels pop out. Sometimes when you are a passenger you can hear a noise when the wheels pop out.

The controllers clear the plane to land and Pilot Ollie gently flies the plane onto the runway. He pushes his toes down on the tops of the pedals and the plane comes to a stop.

Pilot Ollie parks the plane at the airport terminal and Pilot Polly turns the engines off.

When it's nice and safe Pilot Polly tells the cabin crew to open the door and the passengers get off down some steps.

Pilot Polly stands by the steps and waves goodbye to all passengers. Pilot Ollie stays in the flightdeck. He has to get the plane ready and programme the computers for the flight home.